Sarah

Brad

Zach

Mary

Geranium Lady

Joy

Michael

Wumphee

The Geranium Lady Series

The Upside-Down Frown
and Splashes of Joy

A Book About Joy

Barbara Johnson

Illustrations by Victoria Ponikvar Frazier

Thomas Nelson, Inc.

Nashville

Barbara Johnson's
The Geranium Lady Series
The Upside-Down Frown and Splashes of Joy

Text copyright © 1998 by Barbara Johnson
Illustrations copyright © 1998 by Tommy Nelson™,
a division of Thomas Nelson, Inc.

Concept and Story: A. Clayton
Managing Editor: Laura Minchew
Editor: Tama Fortner

Published in Nashville, Tennessee, by Tommy Nelson™,
a division of Thomas Nelson, Inc.

Scripture quoted from the *International Children's Bible, New Century Version*,
copyright © 1986, 1988 by Word Publishing. Used by permission.

Library of Congress Cataloging-in-Publication Data

Johnson, Barbara (Barbara J.)
      The upside-down frown and splashes of joy / Barbara Johnson ;
illustrations by Victoria Ponikvar Frazier.
          p.   cm.—(The Geranium Lady series)
      Summary: Joy and the Geranium Lady use gifts and the sharing of God's love
to brighten the lives of people on a sad and gloomy street. Includes a suggestion
of how to create a paper splash of joy featuring colorful beads and pictures.
      ISBN 0-8499-5844-X
      [1. Christian life—Fiction.] I. Frazier, Victoria Ponikvar, 1966–   ill. II. Title.
III. Series: Johnson, Barbara (Barbara J.). Geranium Lady series.
PZ7.J63035Up   1998
[E]—dc21
                                                                                                98-6488
                                                                                                   CIP
                                                                                                    AC

Printed in the United States of America
98 99 00 01 02 QPH 9 8 7 6 5 4 3 2 1

LETTER TO PARENTS

This isn't the first book I've written about joy! In fact, all of my books—such as *Stick a Geranium in Your Hat and Be Happy!* and *Splashes of Joy in the Cesspools of Life*—deal with the humor and hope we experience when we seek to live a joy-filled life. Only God can fill us to overflow with true joy—one that's much deeper than just a smile or a good attitude.

But how do we explain a concept like this to children and grand-children? Well . . . that's where the idea for this fun, new children's series first popped up. You see, I believe laughter is the sweetest music that ever greeted the human ear. Throughout these pages, my hope is that kids will laugh—and learn some valuable lessons—as they follow the Geranium Lady on her zany adventures.

When we seek God with all our hearts, the "gloomees" don't have a chance. If you want joy for a day, go on a picnic. But if you want joy for life, invest time in others. It's true—shared joy is double joy!

Wishing you splashes of joy,

Barbara Johnson

The Geranium Lady

Knock, Knock. Wiggle, Wiggle. Ding Dong. Head Scratch. Joy giggled at the funny way she had to knock on the Geranium Lady's pink door.

"That's the secret code," the Geranium Lady laughed. "Come in, come in!"

"You have paint all over you," Joy said.

"Yes," the Geranium Lady agreed. "I was painting my house happier colors . . . when I accidentally spilled a bag of marbles into the paint cans and splashed myself with a rainbow of colors!"

The Geranium Lady's newly painted home was filled with bright flowers, loud polka music, the yummy smell of warm cookies, and a dog, Wumphee, who welcomed Joy with big "slurppy" kisses.

"I'm glad you're here," the Geranium Lady said. "I have a special project and could sure use your help."

"This neighborhood is filled with sad faces, unhappy homes . . . even gloomy gardens," said the Geranium Lady. "Let's brighten up these people's day with some surprise visits."

Then with a laugh
and a smile, she added,
"We'll make this day so joyfully fun
it will turn their frowns upside down into smiles."
Joy thought that sounded like a great idea.

"Can we start with Michael? He's been sick for days," Joy said.
The Geranium Lady already had a plan. "Let's surprise him with
something round and gooey that's tasty and chewy!"

When Michael opened the door,
he couldn't believe what he was staring at . . .

. . . a super-gigantic, chocolate chip cookie so big that the Geranium Lady had to hold one side while Joy held the other.

As they snacked on a piece of the huge cookie, Joy and the Geranium Lady shared with Michael how much God loves him.

Next they went to see a girl named Mary. She always seemed sad
... like she had forgotten how to smile. As they knocked on her door,
the Geranium Lady was holding several geranium plants.

When Mary opened the door, the Geranium Lady threw the flowers
up in the air . . .

. . . and started juggling geraniums so fast that her hands and the plants became a blur!

Mary was so tickled by this silly sight that she began to smile.

The Geranium Lady said, "That's why God tells us to be of good cheer—because He's bigger than all the sad things in life!"

Then they walked to Mr. Higgen's home.

"He's the grumpiest man I've ever met," whispered Joy.

The Geranium Lady encouraged Joy to find a way to make this grouchy soul smile.

So when the frown-faced man with bushy eyebrows threw open his door . . .

. . . Joy plopped the Geranium Lady's funny hat right on his balding head. He began to laugh and laugh.

The Geranium Lady said, "See how fast God can turn a frown upside down! That's why I tell people who are sad to stick a geranium in their hat and be happy!"

"This has been so fun," Joy said as they walked down the
sidewalk. "But I wish we had something to leave with people to
remind them of God's love."

With a twinkle in her eye, the Geranium Lady said, "I've got it!
I just thought of what we can give people. Let's hurry back to
my house!"

Joy waited curiously in the kitchen as the Geranium Lady disappeared, only to return a moment later with a bucket. Joy's eyes widened as the Geranium Lady dumped out some of the marbles that had accidentally fallen in the paint cans that morning.

The round, shiny objects were now a paint-splattered mixture of glittering colors. "These are little splashes of joy!" the Geranium Lady said. "We can give these to people to remind them of the many ways God sprinkles their day with joy!"

And that's how Joy and the
Geranium Lady started turning
frowns upside down—by sharing
with others how God brightens our
lives with His splashes of joy.

BE FULL OF JOY IN THE LORD.
Philippians 3:1

MAKE YOUR OWN "SPLASHES OF JOY"!

The real Geranium Lady, Barbara Johnson, gives "Splashes of Joy" to thousands of people each year. Now you can make your own "Splashes of Joy" to give to your friends. It's a great way to remind people that God cares and wants to splash their day with a little joy!

"Splashes of Joy" can be made out of just about anything. Here are some fun ideas to get you started. Be sure your mom or dad helps you with this project!

PAPER "SPLASHES OF JOY"

Cut out fun shapes from colored paper. Draw pictures and designs on the front, and write "JOY" on the back.

You can also cut out circles from thin cardboard (like a cereal box) and then paint them with bright tempera paint. To really make them shine, glue on sparkly beads and glitter.